Miles Away from Home

by Joan Cottle

HARCOURT, INC. • *San Diego New York London*

With special thanks to Allyn, Susan, Deborah, Lynn, and Linda

www.harcourt.com

Library of Congress Cataloging-in-Publication Data
Cottle, Joan.
Miles away from home/by Joan Cottle.
p. cm.
Summary: Although Miles the dog gets into lots of trouble while at the beach with his family, he finally finds a way to make it the best vacation ever.
[1. Dogs—Fiction. 2. Beaches—Fiction. 3. Vacations—Fiction.]
I. Title.
PZ7.C8294Mi 2001
[E]—dc21 99-50609
ISBN 0-15-202212-0

First edition
A C E G H F D B

Printed in Singapore

The illustrations in this book were done in watercolor, colored pencil, and ink on Fabriano Artistico 140 cold press.
The display type was set in Alcoholica.
The text type was set in Esprit.
Printed and bound by Tien Wah Press, Singapore
This book was printed on totally chlorine-free Nymolla Matte Art paper.
Production supervision by Sandra Grebenar and Ginger Boyer
Designed by Linda Lockowitz

For my children,
Kristina and Peter

One day Miles saw an ad for a vacation house in the morning paper. Dad saw the ad, too.

And now here we are, thought Miles.
This will be the best vacation ever.

Miles reviewed water safety rules
and made good use of his new whistle.

Miles, Kristina, and Peter rode perfect waves.

His family built an enormous sand castle.

Miles was in charge of the moat. He liked to help.

Miles helped other people, too.
He put up umbrellas, even when it was windy,

inspected picnic lunches for all four food groups,

and protected children against harmful UV rays.
Miles liked to make new friends.

But sometimes Miles wasn't such a help.

He broke an umbrella, ate a picnic lunch, and used up all the number thirty sunblock.

Miles felt bad. He hated getting in trouble.

So he tried his best
to be good. He played
with the kids. He was a
natural at Frisbee.

He helped Mom with the
cooking. Marinades were his
favorite.

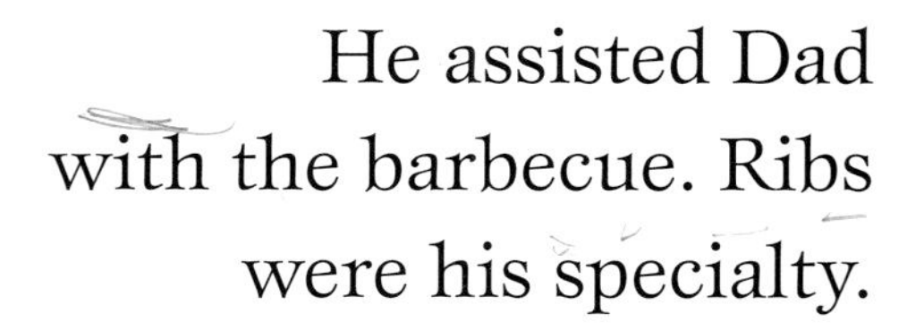

He assisted Dad
with the barbecue. Ribs
were his specialty.

He helped get the kids ready for bed.
Mom read. Miles turned the pages.
Things were just fine.

Miles spent the next morning surfing with his family.

Then he went for ice cream.

Miles liked to share. But he miscalculated how much twenty orange freezy pops would cost.

He didn't have enough money. Miles felt awful. He was in trouble again.

So he tried to be
on his best behavior.
He played Go Fish.
He let the kids win.

He did the laundry. Darks in
cold, whites in hot.

He reviewed hurricane
evacuation procedures. He
checked all the batteries.

He brushed his teeth before bed.
He even flossed. Miles felt much better.

The next day Miles and his family went to the Ocean Side Putt-Putt Course.

Miles excelled at miniature golf. He had a steady paw and a good eye. He even gave Dad a few tips.

On the last hole he helped Peter with a tricky shot.

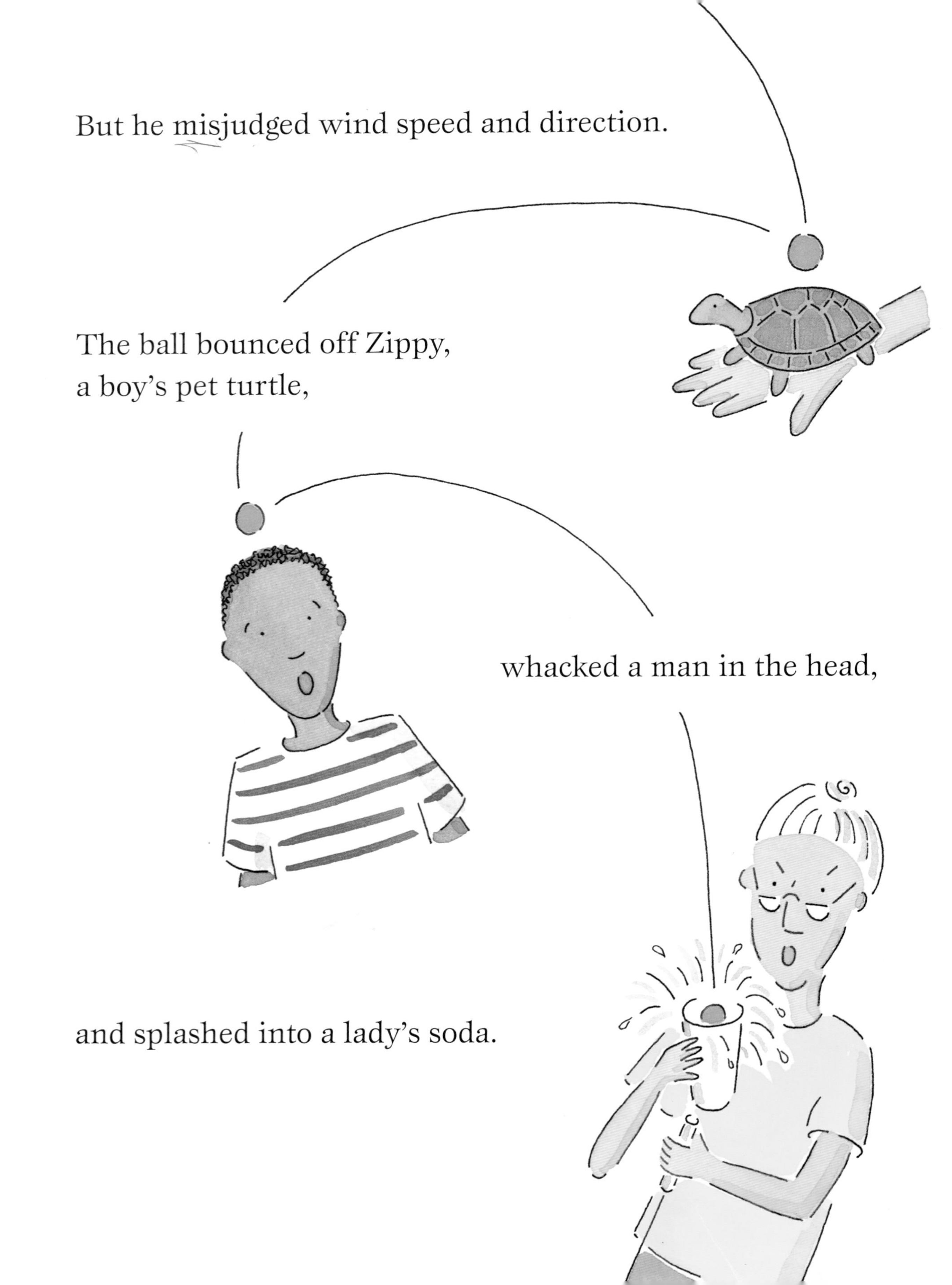

But he misjudged wind speed and direction.

The ball bounced off Zippy,
a boy's pet turtle,

whacked a man in the head,

and splashed into a lady's soda.

“That dog should be in a kennel,” said the manager.
But I was only trying to help, thought Miles.

Miles felt terrible. That night he skipped dessert and went to bed early.

Maybe I should be in a kennel, thought Miles.

Miles curled up with Dad's slippers and tried to get some sleep. He tossed and turned. He dreamed about the kennel: smelly wet cement floors, locks with no keys, roommates named Spike—and even worse, lonely nights without his family.

No one to tuck me in, thought Miles. *No one to scratch my tummy. I would be all alone.*

The next morning Miles didn't feel like swimming.
He stayed behind on his towel.
Maybe this isn't a great vacation after all.

He stared out at the ocean.

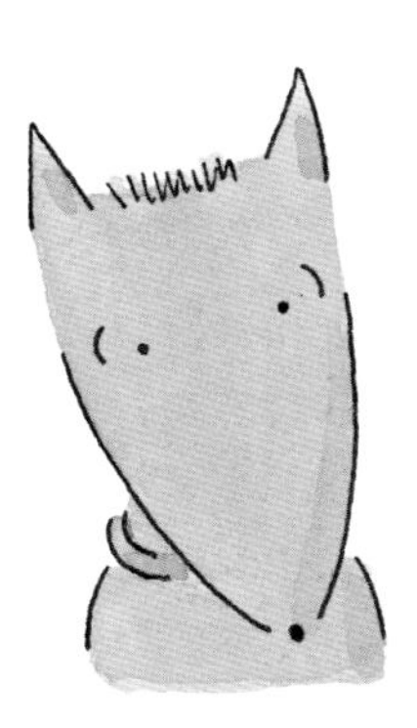

He saw a lady in the water.
Suddenly she grabbed her leg.
"Ouch!" said the lady. "My leg!"

Oh no, thought Miles. *She has a cramp. She needs help!*

Miles knew what he had to do. He blew his whistle.

He grabbed a flotation device, sprinted across the beach, and jumped into the surf.

He swam freestyle.

He swam backstroke.

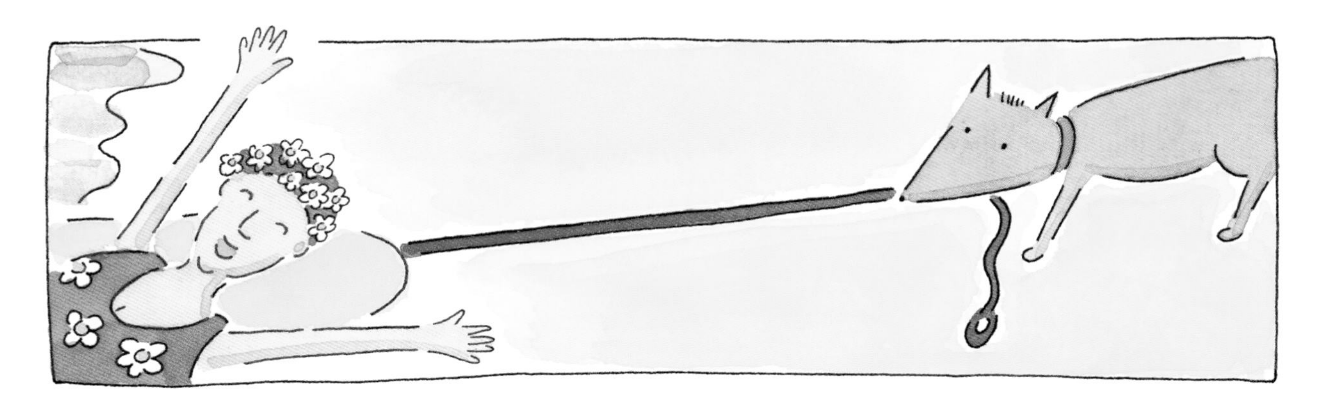

He pulled the lady to shore.
It was a perfect rescue.

And everyone knew it. Even Miles.

Miles became an honorary lifeguard,
and he got to sit in the lifeguard chair.

His family threw a big party to celebrate.

It was the best vacation ever.